Look and Find

Mother Goose

and
Her Nursery-Rhyme Friends

Old Woman in the Shoe
London Bridge • Old King Cole
Jack and Jill • And more!

Illustrated by Bob Terrio

Cover illustrated by Bob Terrio and Jerry Tiritilli

Illustration Assistant: Gale Terrio

Illustration script development by Christina Wilsdon

Louis Weber, C.E.O.
Publications International, Ltd.
7373 North Cicero Avenue
Lincolnwood, Illinois 60646

Manufactured in the U.S.A.

8 7 6 5 4 3 2 1

ISBN 1-56173-418-7

PUBLICATIONS INTERNATIONAL, LTD.

Mary had a little lamb;
   its fleece was white as snow.
And everywhere that Mary went,
   the lamb was sure to go!

Mary's lamb followed her to school today. Things got pretty wild and wooly around there! After you find Mother Goose, look for these other folks at Mary's school.

Mother Goose

Mary

Mary's little lamb

Mama Sheep

The sheepdog

The teacher

The principal

The crossing guard

There was an old woman who lived in a shoe.
She had so many children, she didn't know what to do!

Mother Goose is on her way to help out with the kids. Just wait until she learns that each child has lost a shoe! First, find Mother Goose. Then help her look for these missing shoes.

— Mother Goose

— A tennis shoe

— A cowboy boot

— A bunny slipper

— A saddle shoe

— A rain boot

— A summer sandal

— An ice skate

H umpty Dumpty sat on a wall.
Humpty Dumpty had a great fall.
All the king's horses and all the
   king's men
Couldn't put Humpty together again!

Mother Goose has made a special glue.
Can you find her? Can you find these
characters who will help her mend
Humpty Dumpty?

— Mother Goose

— Dr. Omelette

— Mr. Egg Foo Yung

— Nog, the St. Bernard

— Eggs Benedict Arnold

— Monsieur L'Oeuf

— Señor Huevos

— Dr. Egghead

— Nurse Egglantine

London Bridge is falling down,
  falling down, falling down.
London Bridge is falling down,
  my fair lady!

London Bridge is teetering and
tottering! First, find Mother Goose.
Then help her find these things so she
can lend a hand in building it up again.

Mother Goose

This hammer

A saw

A level

A barrel of nails

Safety goggles

Work gloves

A drill

A screwdriver

Little Boy Blue, come, blow
your horn!
Bo-Peep's sheep are in meadow—
your cows are in the corn!

Little Boy Blue and Little Bo-Peep
are sleeping on the job! Find Mother
Goose and the two sleepyheads. Then
help her find these things lost in
the meadow.

Mother Goose

Little Boy Blue

Little Bo-Peep

Bo-Peep's crook

Boy Blue's horn

A sheepdog

An alarm clock

12 lambs' tails

O ld King Cole and the Queen
    of Hearts
Called for fiddlers and baked
    some tarts.
They served blackbird pie to one
    and all,
When a cat appeared in the royal hall.
The birds stopped singing and all
    flew away;
And a knave stole the tarts at the end of
    the day!

The party's over! Can you find these
guests before they leave?

Mother Goose

Old King Cole

Queen of Hearts

Fiddler 1

Fiddler 2

Fiddler 3

The pussy-cat

The Knave of Hearts

Jack and Jill went up the hill
to fetch a pail of water.
Jack fell down and broke his crown,
and Jill came tumbling after!

Mother Goose led the rescue party up the hill. Can you find her and these other rescuers?

Mother Goose

Dr. Patchwell

The King of Tumbletown

Head Mistress Dob

Rescue Rover

First-Aid Kit

Mayor Noggin

Dizzy and Lizzy

There was a crooked man
  who walked a crooked mile.
He found a crooked sixpence
  beside a crooked stile.
He bought a crooked cat
  that caught a crooked mouse,
And they all lived together
  in a little crooked house!

Where's Mother Goose in this crazy place? Can you find these crooked characters, too?

— Mother Goose

— The crooked man

The crooked cat

The crooked mouse

A crooked dog

A crooked cow

A crooked snake

A crooked crook

BENT BROTHERS CIRCUS

LOOP·THE·LOOP

WATER

OLIVER TWIST

BENT BLVD.

RIPPLE RD.

WELCOME TO TWISTERTOWN

PAINT

Tｈis book has ended,
   and now it's time
To look for more than
   just one rhyme.
Let's take a stroll with
   Mother Goose
And see what rhymes are
   on the loose!

After you find Mother Goose, look for
these nursery rhymes!

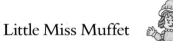

— Mother Goose

— Little Jack Horner

— Mary, Mary, Quite Contrary

— Little Miss Muffet

— Old Mother Hubbard

— Jack Be Nimble

— Pat-a-Cake

— Hey, Diddle, Diddle

TO ST. IVES

MALT

JACK

TO GLOUCESTER

DR. FOSTER

Moby Dick

MARKET

BARBER

BUTCHER

BAKER

CANDLESTICK MAKER

GONE FISHING

GONE FISHING

GONE FISHING

WOOL

PICKLED PEPPERS FOR PICKING

EGGS

Go back to Mary's school to find these classroom things:

☐ A spinning globe
☐ The teacher's pet
☐ The class "bull"-y
☐ An apple for the teacher
☐ A pencil sharpener
☐ A spelling "bee"
☐ The class clown

Go back to the site of Humpty Dumpty's fall. Can you find these animals that lay eggs?

☐ A duck
☐ A snail
☐ A snake
☐ A crocodile
☐ A spider
☐ A fish
☐ A frog
☐ An ostrich
☐ A penguin
☐ A butterfly

Go back to the Old Woman's shoe-house. Can you find these children who are missing a shoe?

☐ A basketball player
☐ A tennis player
☐ A cowboy
☐ A sleepyhead
☐ A cheerleader
☐ A puddle jumper
☐ A beach bum
☐ A hippie
☐ An ice skater

Go back to the crooked town. Can you find these straight things?

☐ A straight jacket
☐ Ducks in a row
☐ A straight face
☐ A beeline
☐ A straight shooter
☐ "As the crow flies"
☐ "Straight as an arrow"